GRATITUDE ★ the ★ GREAT

Written by Pamelyn Rocco

Illustrated by Taylor Barron

the collective
BOOK STUDIO

So, I have super cool news . . .

My cousin Hope is finally coming to visit us all the way from Brazil!

A year is a long time to go without your best friend.

I guess all of those

penny-throw wishes paid off.

That's one of the rituals we do as a family.

Every time we see a fountain we take a penny and say:

Thank you, dear Penny,

Your kindness is key

In helping my wishes come back to me!

Gramma B calls these things *rituals* because we do the same thing every single time.

Gramma B is the coolest.

She teaches me how to sew,

plays video games,

and lets me stay up late

for disco music dance parties

(*shhh,* don't tell my parents).

Pillow Chat is my favorite ritual. My whole family—including Gramma's pet lizard, Zima—sits in my room at bedtime and takes turns saying what we are grateful for and why. Gramma says that the *why* is the most important part. We hold Gramma's special heart-shaped crystal when it is our turn. She says it has special powers.

Last night I shared how I was grateful for my dad. Why? For making me the best

mohawk skateboard helmet ever—just like the Greek warriors in my favorite story!

Finally, Hope is here! I run into the living room,
and we immediately do our secret handshake.
The Pound-with-Fireworks, Spin, Hi-Five, Low-Five,
Two Snaps, Arm Slide, Peace Sign Handshake
(*shhh,* don't tell anyone).

I am so pumped to show her my helmet.

"Look, Hope, I'm officially a warrior on wheels.

And there's a surprise for you, too!"

"Oh, thank you, Gramma B!" squeals Hope. "I have always wanted one of your special hats."

Gramma B smiles. "I know you did, darling. I made it extra fabulous just for you."

My mom surprises us with our favorite breakfast, banana chocolate-chip name pancakes.
In between bites, I notice Hope's bracelets. "Are those new?" I ask her.

"Aren't they the best? I make them with my grandmother in
São Paulo," she explains.

"We call them Rea bracelets because that was my great-great-grandmother's nickname. She started making them with her kids to remind them of all the things they have to be grateful for. Everyone says they have special powers!" Hope explains.

"Are you thinking what I'm thinking?" she asks. I laugh, and we both run to grab Gramma B's craft box full of string and beads.

Hope is a good teacher. "First, think of who or what you are grateful for. See this blue and yellow one? I made it to remind myself of the fun I have at the beach in Ilhabela," she smiles. "Next, pick the string and bead colors. There are a bunch of different ways you can make Reas, so just be creative. My favorite is tying the knots together like this and adding colorful beads. But we *always* put a bead on the end with an R on it to make it extra special."

My first Rea bracelet is for Hope, of course. Hope makes a sparkly one for Gramma B, to thank her for the hat. Before we know it, we have, like, a million bracelets. Some for our family, teachers, friends, coaches, and even people we don't know yet. And, man, are they cool!

We are so proud. We give one to everyone in the family. "Hope, these bracelets are very special. Thank you for teaching us about your new family traditions," says Mom, smiling.

Then Dad asks if we want to take a stroll on the Venice Boardwalk. It's one of *our* Saturday afternoon traditions.

"Yes!" I scream and make my biggest fist pump.

"Woo hoo," squeals Gramma B.

"Let's roll," says Hope as she grabs the rest of the Reas.

I sure missed having someone to sit with in the back of our van. Mom is right—the smallest things can make us happy.

There is always something crazy cool going on at the boardwalk.
It is my favorite spot in the world.

"Wow, I sure missed this place. I love how different everyone is," Hope says.

"And check out all of the creative things they are doing," I add.

"Well . . ." Hope holds out the box in her hands. "I did bring the Reas we made."

"Are you thinking what I'm thinking?" I ask.

Hope laughs. "Yes! We should definitely give some away today."

"Hi, Mister. I wanted to give you this bracelet

because I think your hair is totally rad, and I love your music!"

Hope smiles at a girl on roller skates. "I like your moves. Thank you for putting on a fun show. This bracelet is for you."

People seem to really like them. We get hi-fives, fist bumps, and a bunch of big smiles. It makes us both feel . . . *special.*

Before we know it, people start lining up

to see what we are handing out. Then a really nice,

fancy-looking lady comes up to us. "Hello there. I'm curious.

What are you giving to everyone that brings such big smiles to their faces?"

We explain the whole story behind our Reas (even the special powers part).

"It sounds like giving a Rea feels as good as getting one!

We need more of this in the world," says the Fancy Lady, smiling.

"If it's okay with you two, I would love to share your story with my friends. Even grown-ups need a reminder of how great it feels to give—and receive—gratitude."

"I'd really like that," says Hope with a big smile.

I find the fanciest Rea in the box and say, "Ma'am, this one is for you, for being so kind to us."

She smiles, touches my mohawk, and says, "Well, aren't you a warrior of gratitude. I'm going to call you **Gratitude the Great**!"

I like the sound of that.

By the time we get home, we are all over the Internet.

"Holy moly," Gramma B keeps saying.

"This is nuts," giggles my mom.

"Best day ever," I tell Hope.

We are exhausted, and it is finally time for Pillow Chat. Dad is the last one to share. "I'm grateful to have a rad family to share adventures like today with." He gets a silly grin on his face. "And speaking of adventures, I hope you guys are up for another one ... in ... *New York City!*"

I guess some big news channel saw the Fancy Lady's video and wants to interview us about the Reas.

"I'll pack the bracelets," Hope squeals.

"I'll bring the crystal," says Gramma B.

"I'll wear my helmet," I say.

"And from now on you can call me **GRATITUDE THE GREAT**!"

Dear Reader,

Modern research shows that teaching a gratitude practice to our kids has significant benefits: increased positive mood, optimism, hope, resiliency, enthusiasm, and happiness. Being able to mindfully acknowledge what we are thankful for and happy about increases both empathy and kindness to others and even improves physical health while decreasing stress. As an Optimism Doctor®, I believe that being able to teach our kids and help them to make a positive ritual of gratitude in their early lives is key. The beautiful message in this book, *Gratitude the Great,* is such an effective and powerful way to bring the practice of gratitude into your family and into your home.

Things Are Looking Up,

Dr. Deepika Chopra

Optimism Doctor®

Dr. Deepika Chopra holds a doctorate in clinical health psychology and currently practices as an Optimism Doctor®, Visual Imagery Expert & Happiness Researcher, and is the founder of Things Are Looking Up—a place for optimism. She has been a speaker at In Goop Health, Create & Cultivate, and IMPACT and has been a brand partner with companies like Fisher-Price for mindful parenting, BeautyCounter, Rae wellness, and more. She conducts optimism sessions and teaches a number of signature workshops all over the world.

@drdeepikachopra
@allthingsarelookingup

"Gratitude is not only the greatest of virtues, but the parent of all the others."—Cicero

I think of gratitude as the greatest natural superpower that anyone—no matter age, race, religion, gender, or social status—can use, practice, and hold in their pockets forever. So, how do we instill this into the daily lives of our families?

To start, gratitude is best caught, not taught. Gratitude needs to become a ritual, a habit as common as breakfast in the morning or books at bedtime. When rituals are practiced at an early age, they are never forgotten. So, here are a few tips to incorporate gratitude into your family's daily lives:

1. Pillow Chat. Establish a special tradition that your family does together that prompts your child to be mindful of people, objects, and experiences in daily life. It can be as simple as having her draw what she was grateful for once a week and explain why. Because the WHY is the most important part! Collect the drawings into a small book that you can look through every few months..

2. Gratitude Train. This activity allows children of all ages to recognize that the things they have don't just appear but that they come from someone or something other than themselves. For example, talk about the people and things responsible for dinner—from the seeds that are planted in the ground, to the rain that helps the crops grow, to the farmer who picks the crops, to the grocery store that sells those crops, to the adults who work hard to buy the food at the grocery store, and finally, to the hands that prepare the meal.

3. Thank Yous. Even if your child can't write yet, he can still be a part of the process. The key is to have fun and not make the practice of gratitude a chore. Take the time to hand-deliver the notes. That way kids can see the joy their appreciation brings.

Remember gratitude is FREE to the entire universe, so let's use it!

For more free stuff, including activities, practices, and the science and research behind gratitude, visit www.gratitudethegreat.com and follow @gratitudethegreat. You will be so grateful you did.

Pamelyn Rocco

To Chris, Moorea, and Harlow:
You have given me more joy than
I ever imagined was possible.
Thank you for being my constant reminder
of what I have to be grateful for.

To my family and friends:
There is a piece of all of you in this story.
Thank you for inspiring me.

Text and illustration copyright © 2021 Pamelyn Rocco

All rights reserved. No part of this book may be reproduced in
any form without written permission from the publisher.

Library of Congress Cataloging-in-Publication information available.
ISBN-13: 978-1-951412-02-9

Manufactured in China

Design and illustrations by Taylor Barron

10 9 8 7 6 5 4 3 2 1

The Collective Book Studio
Oakland, CA
Thecollectivebook.studio